Ant and Honey Bee
What a Pair!

Megan McDonald

illustrated by G. Brian Karas

CANDLEWICK PRESS
CAMBRIDGE, MASSACHUSETTS

from:
CRICKET
to:
Ant and Honey Bee

Text copyright © 2005 by Megan McDonald
Illustrations copyright © 2005 by G. Brian Karas

First edition 2005

Library of Congress Cataloging-in-Publication Data

McDonald, Megan.
Ant and Honey Bee / Megan McDonald ; illustrated by G. Brian Karas. —1st ed.
p. cm.
Summary: Ant and Honey Bee try to come up with original outfits
for a costume party and almost experience disaster.
ISBN 0-7636-1265-0
[1. Costume—Fiction. 2. Ants—Fiction. 3. Honeybee—Fiction. 4. Bees—Fiction.
5. Parties—Fiction.] I. Karas, G. Brian, ill. II. Title.
PZ7.M478419 An 2001
[E]—dc21   00-037888

2 4 6 8 10 9 7 5 3 1

Printed in Singapore

This book was typeset in Usherwood.
The illustrations were done in gouache, acrylic, and pencil.

Candlewick Press
2067 Massachusetts Avenue
Cambridge, Massachusetts 02140

visit us at www.candlewick.com

For Judi Ingram Adkins
M. M.

For Ben and Sam
G. B. K.

Ant was getting antsy. She stared out the window at the gray clouds. Only a few hours left till Cricket's costume party.

"What can we be for the dress-up party?" she asked her friend Honey Bee.

"Pilgrims," said Honey Bee.

"Pilgrims! But we've been pilgrims for two years in a row," said Ant. "Pilgrims are boring."

"Then be an ear of corn, if it will make you happy," said Honey Bee.

"What will you be if I'm an ear of corn?" Ant asked.

"I'll be a bee," said Honey Bee.

"But you *are* a bee!" Ant said. "You can't just be you."

"It's good to be yourself," said Honey Bee.

"You can be that anytime," said Ant. "I know. Let's be a pair."

"I'll be the pear and you be the stem," said Honey Bee.

"Not that kind of pear!" said Ant. "A two-things-that-go-together kind of pair."

"Then I'll be an anteater," said Honey Bee,
"and you be the ant."

"Too scary!" said Ant.

Ant thought and thought about things that go together.

She looked in the kitchen. Peanut butter and jelly?

She looked in the bathroom. Toilet paper and toilet?

She looked in the laundry room.

"I know!" she said. "Let's be a washer and dryer!"

"A washer and dryer make a good pair," said Honey Bee.

"Yippee! No more pilgrims!"

Ant and Honey Bee found two boxes
that were just the right size. Ant cut
holes for legs and a big hole for her head
in one box. Honey Bee cut holes for legs
and wings, and a big hole for her head,
in the other box.

Ant and Honey Bee made knobs and
dials. Ant drew soapsuds down the front
of her washer.

Honey Bee glued fuzzy
cotton balls for lint on her
dryer. They worked as hard
as two ants in an anthill. They worked as
hard as two bees in a beehive.

"BLUB! BLUB!"

said Ant, just like a washer
when it washes clothes.

"BUZZZZZZ!"

said Honey Bee, just like a dryer when it's done drying.

"We make the best washer and dryer!" said Ant.
"We make the best pair!" said Honey Bee.

It was time for Cricket's party. When Ant tried
to walk down the front steps, she could hardly
move her legs. When Honey Bee tried to walk
down the sidewalk, she could not see where
she was going.

"It's hard to walk when you're a washer,"
said Ant.

"It's hard to see when you're a dryer,"
said Honey Bee.

The wind blew Ant and Honey Bee
down the street, where they bumped
into Beetle and Fly.

"Look! Two dice!" said Beetle.

"No, it's a couple of ice cubes!" said Fly.

"Blub! Blub!" said Ant, so everyone would know she was a washer.

"Buzzzzz," said Honey Bee, so everyone would know she was a dryer.

"Hey! Swiss cheese!" called Butterfly.

"Yum! Yum! Are those moth holes?" asked Moth.

"Show them your spin cycle, Ant," said Honey Bee.

"Show them your tumble dry," said Ant.

Ant spun around in circles. "Blub! Blub!"

Honey Bee bounced up and down.

"Buzzzzz!"

They spun and bounced
all the way down the hill,
where they ran into the Spiders.

"Look! It's a stove and a dishwasher!"
said Old Man Spider.
"No, honey," said Mrs. Spider.
"Can't you see — it's two computers."

"Dancing computers. Very
clever!" said Old Man Spider.

"No one knows *what* we are," said
Honey Bee.

"Mr. and Mrs. Spider thought we were
clever," said Ant.

"No. They thought dancing computers
were clever," said Honey Bee.

Just then, a gust of wind blew up.
Then, *plip.*

Plip.

Plip,

plip,

PLIP!

"Oh, no! Rain!" cried Ant. "Run!"
"We can't run," said Honey Bee. "We
can hardly walk!"

Ant and Honey Bee waddled through the pouring rain, all the way to Cricket's party.

"My washer is leaking!"
said Ant.

"My dryer is all wet!"
said Honey Bee.

Ant and Honey Bee did not look like a washer and dryer. They did not even look like dice or ice cubes or computers. They did not look like a two-things-that-go-together pair.

They looked like soggy blobs of wet cardboard. A couple of mud pies.

Ant and Honey Bee dragged themselves
up the steps, one, two, three, to Cricket's
front door. Ant was not going *Blub, blub.*
Honey Bee was not going *Buzzzz.*

Cricket opened the door. "No pilgrims
this year?"

"No," said Ant.

"No," said Honey Bee.

"So what are you?" Cricket asked.

Ant looked at Honey Bee.
Honey Bee looked at Ant.

Maybe Honey Bee's soggy cardboard
lump did not look so lumpy.
   Maybe Ant's soggy cardboard blob did
not look so blobby.

"She's a — BEEHIVE!" said Ant.

Honey Bee smiled. "And she's an ANTHILL!"

"Creative!" said Cricket. "What a pair!"